The Spark Files

Terry Deary trained as an actor before turning to writing full-time. He has many successful fiction and non-fiction children's books to his name, and is rarely out of the best-seller charts.

Barbara Allen trained and worked as a teacher and is now a full-time researcher for the Open University.

The Spark Files

Book Three

Shock Tactics

illustrated by Philip Reeve

faber and faber

First published in 1998
by Faber and Faber Limited
3 Queen Square London WCIN 3AU

Typeset by Faber and Faber Ltd
Printed in England by Mackays of Chatham plc, Chatham, Kent

Cover design: Shireen Nathoo

Terry Deary and Barbara Allen are hereby identified as authors
of this work in accordance with Section 77 of the Copyright,
Designs and Patents Act 1988

A CIP record for this book
is available from the British Library

ISBN 0-571-19370-6

10 9 8 7 6 5 4 3 2 1

For my son, Edward, with love. BA

BE A SAFE SCIENTIST

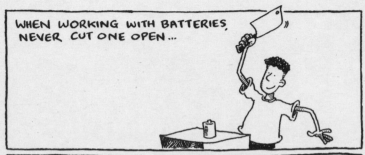

WHEN WORKING WITH BATTERIES, NEVER CUT ONE OPEN...

...OR PUT IT IN YOUR MOUTH

ALWAYS STORE THEM WITH THE TERMINALS APART SO THAT THEY DON'T SHORT CIRCUIT

THROW AWAY OLD BATTERIES, ESPECIALLY IF THEY ARE LEAKING...

Shock Tactics

File 1

Simon Spark
(that's me!)

They call me Simple Simon,
I can't think why. I am not as stupid
as I look! I am kind, helpful, handsome...
and modest.

Give three cheers for Simon Spark
Lots of brains and lots of guts
Top computer ace of Duckpool
Leader of the Internuts
(That's our after-school computer club)

File 2

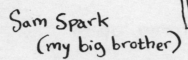

Sam Spark
(my big brother)

He's really lucky to have a kid brother like me. I keep him right and use my ace computer skills to help him with his homework.

Brother Sam's a cheerful lad
Laughs at this, that and the
other

Not too good at doing homework
Lucky he's got a clever brother.

(That's me by the way.)

File 3

Granny Spark.

  She's so old that even her wrinkles have wrinkles. She had so many candles on her last birthday cake we barbecued the ceiling.

Granny Spark's an O.A.P.
Brain as sharp as any toothpick
Drives around in her old banger
Think she swapped it for her
                    broomstick

(Dad says.)

File 4

Cedric Crump.

Caretaker at Duckpool School. Kids like to hang his photo over their bedroom door to keep vampires away. That's how ugly he is.

Every school must have a Cedric
Like our own school's Mister Crump.
Floors and windows shine like mirrors
Pity he is such a grump
('specially if you drop a crisp packet)

File 5

Headmaster
Macbeth

Headteacher of Duckpool School. Always wears a suit. Never teaches kids in case he gets it dirty or gets chalk on it.

Our headmaster drives a jag
Wears silk ties and dazzling socks
Wants to have the best school ever
Shame the kids are thick as blocks

(Well, some of them)

Chapter 1

Duckpool School is old. My gran went to Duckpool School . . . and she's older than William the Conker, the man who won the Battle of Trafalgar Square. (Least, that's what Dad says, but he was never good at History.) Anyway, Duckpool School is old.

Smoke-blackened, crumbling and smelly . . . and that's just the teachers. Teachers like old Miss Trout. All that trouble began one Monday morning in her lesson. 'Next week,' she said with a yellow-toothed smile, clutching her mud-coloured cardigan excitedly, 'you sit your SATs!'

Everyone looked blank. Nothing unusual there with our class.

'Don't you mean we sit on our seats?' I asked. Teachers sometimes need a little help and I was only trying to help her.

Miss Trout glared at me. I think they teach teachers how to do 'The Glare' in college. 'No, Simon Spark. I mean what I say. You will be taking tests in Maths, English and Science. These tests are called SATs.'

'Why?' Myrtle Brick asked.

Miss Trout's mouth flapped like a goldfish – or a trout – and she said, 'Because they *are*. The point is we need to spend a bit of time practising so you all get top marks!'

'Why?' Myrtle asked again. Myrtle doesn't say much but she likes to know these things.

'Because all of your marks will be added together and Duckpool School gets a score. Then we go into a sort of "Top Ten" to see which is the best school in Wasteland County.'

'Why?'

'So parents can see which is the best school in the area to send their children! Every year they announce a top ten.'

Before Myrtle could ask 'Why?' I called, 'What number were we in last year's top ten?'

Miss Trout blushed a little. 'Eleven,' she muttered.

'How many schools are there in Wasteland?' I asked.

'Eleven,' she admitted. 'But this year we are going to do better!'

'Why?' Myrtle asked.

'Because our new headteacher, Mr Macbeth, says so. He says the only way is up!' We all looked up to the ceiling where she was pointing. There was a flickering light bulb up there that sizzled and went 'Splutt!' A bit like Mr Macbeth's dreams, I guessed.

'Miss, the light bulb's blown, Miss!' Elvis Smith told her.

'Yes, I can see that, Elvis,' Miss Trout said sweetly. 'I will ask Mr Crump the Caretaker to change it. But since light bulbs run on electricity, we may as well start our new science topic this morning. Before your SATs you'll be studying Electricity!'

'Great!' I said. I've always been enthusiastic like that. 'Can I use electricity to bring a monster to life like Professor Frankenstein?' I asked.

'Not this week,' Miss Trout said faintly.

'I could make you an electric chair, Miss!' Elvis Smith offered.

The teacher glared at him. 'Your attempts at humour are misplaced, Elvis,' she said sternly.

'You what?' he blinked.

'You will do this experiment from page ten of your textbooks, *Science for Dunces*,' she said and looked around the classroom for someone she could trust. There was no one. She sighed. 'Myrtle Brick, you are science monitor today. Get the balloons out of the cupboard and give them out.'

'Why?' Myrtle asked.

'Because you'll need them for this experiment,' the teacher replied. 'Now get on quietly while I find Mr Crump.'

We opened our science books and looked at the experiments while Myrtle wiped her nose on her sleeve and set off in search of the balloons. The experiment was quite good fun, even if *Science for Dunces* is the saddest book in the history of school text books. Try it if you like . . .

Sticky Balloons

Here's a jolly game you can play with your friends!
First, each person blow up a balloon. (Be very careful. If you are frightened of big bangs then let an adult do this for you!) Stroke the balloon several times against a woollen jumper.

**Hold the balloon against the wall and let it go.
The balloon should stick to the wall.
Isn't that too amazing for words, children?
Rubbing the balloon against the wool puts a
charge of 'Static Electricity' on its skin. The
wall has a different charge so the wall attracts it.
Remember: 'Opposites attract'. Just like your
mummy and daddy.**

**How long does your balloon stay on the wall? At
a party you can cover a wall with balloons.
Wouldn't that be jolly?**

'Where do I get a woollen jumper?' Elvis asked

'Cross a kangaroo with a sheep,' I muttered.

When the ceiling was covered in balloons we sat and
looked at them. 'Boring,' Elvis said.

'It says in the book it's jolly!' I reminded him.

He looked at me through his narrow eyes and I knew
he had one of his evil ideas. 'What would be really *jolly*
would be to use them for target practice and burst them!'
He turned to Myrtle Brick. 'Get the paper-clips and elastic
bands from Miss Trout's desk.'

'Why?'

'So you're the one who gets into trouble if we get caught!' he cackled.

Myrtle nodded and did as she was told. A minute later the room sounded like a machine-gun battle as balloons popped and flopped to the floor. It was just my luck that the door opened, my elastic band slipped and the paper-clip smacked Miss Trout between the eyes. 'One hour's detention, Simon Spark,' she hissed.

An old man with eyes like a startled beetle, hair like a dirty mop and skin like a dead rhino, stood behind her. 'Look at my floor!' he croaked. It was Mr Crump the caretaker. 'I'm not clearing that mess up after you lot! I'm not! I'm not!'

'Simon Spark can clear it up during his detention,' Miss Trout said. 'The rest of you should be ashamed of yourselves,' she sniffed. 'Class dismiss.'

'Ashamed,' Mr Crump agreed as my class-mates trailed past him. 'When I was at school we'd have been caned for that. Maybe even strung up from the ceiling by the thumbs! Strung up from the ceiling!'

'It was all Simon's idea,' Elvis Smith said as he sidled out of the room and home to an early tea.

That left me alone in the nearly deserted school. And it was the start of the greatest adventure of my life . . .

Chapter 2

Being in detention is no fun when you're on your own. You can't even make rude noises to entertain your friends. I dragged myself out of my seat and wandered around the classroom looking for things to do. I walked past the hamster's cage but, as usual, Spike the hamster was asleep.

There was nothing else to do but collect the balloons that were scattered over the floor. As I threw them into the bin I noticed a piece of headed notepaper sticking out from under an envelope. Now you know that children aren't supposed to read the teachers' letters. I took the letter out of the bin because I was worried that Miss Trout had thrown something away by mistake. Honest!

Wasteland Local Education Authority

The Tall Offices, Edge of Town, Duckpool, DK3 6XZ

Tel & Fax: 01253 778811

Memo to all teachers

This year's SAT papers will arrive at your school soon. We would like to remind all teachers that no cheating is to take place in this year's tests. Other schools, in other areas, do the following disgraceful things:

1. Teachers read the test papers before the day of the tests.

2. Teachers teach the children answers to the questions that are on the papers.

3. Teachers tell the children the answers during the tests.

4. Teachers alter the children's answers.

5. Teachers give the children extra time to do the papers.

We in Wasteland would never do such things!

Donald Duckmouse

Donald Duckmouse
Director.

All the other schools in Duckpool are doing it! No wonder we're bottom of the league!

It would be no good Miss Trout trying to help us with the answers, she'd probably get them wrong.

'It's a bit much when you've got to tell the teachers not to cheat,' I said to Spike. The hamster snored and rolled on his back.

The footsteps in the corridor sounding like Grumpy Crumpy so I dropped to my knees and started polishing the floor with my handkerchief. Then I heard a second set of footsteps and a man spoke. 'Ah, Mr Cramp, just the person I was looking for.'

'What do you want?' asked Grumpy.

I crawled to the door, opened it a little and looked through the gap. The man wore a suit in a shiny, grey material. His red tie was covered in dazzling golden suns – nearly as dazzling as his great white grin. It was the new headteacher, Mr Macbeth. He'd just arrived that day and had grinned his way around the school, being charming to parents. He went around patting children on the head then wiping his hand on a black silk handkerchief.

As he stepped out of his red Jaguar sports car that

morning I noticed his green socks had purple frogs on them.

'Now where are we going to put these new computers I've just bought?' Headmaster Macbeth asked.

'There's no room for them, not an inch,' Crump grumped.

'Nonsense. I'm sure we can find somewhere.'

'The school is full of stuff already and there's no space for any more rubbish. Rubbish everywhere. Everywhere! And you should see the state of the staff teacups. Poisonous! Poisonous!'

'Computers are the future, Mr Crump. I'm sure you realize that. We must give the dear children every opportunity to succeed. I have a dream, Mr Crump! A dream that each child will be linked to every other child in the world. Finding space is just a little hurdle we must conquer.' (Why didn't he just say, 'Crump, find me a room or you're sacked.' It would have been much quicker.)

'I'm too old to go jumping over hurdles,' the old man complained.

'What about this room next to Miss Trout's classroom?' asked the Head. 'It's only got cleaning stuff in it.'

What Mr Macbeth didn't know was that that was Grumpy's room.

'You can't use that room. I say, you can't use that! It can't be done.'

'There's no such word as "can't",' said Mr Macbeth.

(Don't adults say some stupid things? When I go out my Gran says, 'If you get run over by a bus and come home dead, I'll murder you.')

I heard the ring of a mobile phone and Mr Macbeth answering it. 'I'll be late tonight, darling. The new computers arrived today and I haven't a clue how to set them up!'

When I heard that I jumped to my feet and flung the door open. 'Mr Macbeth! I'm Simon Spark, and I'm your man!'

'No you're not, you're a kid!' Crump cried. 'A rotten kid!'

'I am a highly experienced computer operator!' I said.

Mr Macbeth grinned till his face almost split. His white teeth lit up the gloomy corridor. 'There's no time like the present!' he said. 'Let's get started.'

Mr Crump complained and whinged and snapped and snarled, but he also carried and carted computers into the room he called his 'Cubby Hole'. In half an hour the computers and printers were set up. Half an hour later I was connected to a phone line and we were in touch with millions of other computers through the Internet.

'Show me how it works,' the headteacher demanded.

It was a good chance to do my homework so I started to search for information on electricity.

I found it in no time.

STATIC ELECTRICITY

STATIC ELECTRICITY IS AN ELECTRIC CHARGE THAT STANDS STILL. IT DOESN'T MOVE IN A CURRENT. THE ANCIENT GREEK THALES DISCOVERED ELECTRICITY IN ABOUT 600 BC. HE RUBBED A PIECE OF AMBER WITH CLOTH. THE AMBER THEN ATTRACTED SMALL OBJECTS. HERE'S AN EXPERIMENT YOU CAN TRY- BUT THALES COULDN'T.

BENDING WATER

1. RUB A PLASTIC COMB WITH A WOOLLEN JUMPER.
2. TURN ON THE TAP JUST ENOUGH TO MAKE A THIN STREAM OF WATER.
3. HOLD THE COMB NEAR THE WATER.
4. YOU SHOULD SEE THE WATER BEND TOWARDS THE COMB. IT HAS BEEN ATTRACTED BY THE STATIC ELECTRICITY.

I printed out the information and packed up my bag ready to go home. 'I'm glad we've got such keen and intelligent children in this school,' Mr Macbeth said as he turned and strode down the corridor. 'See you tomorrow. I'll leave you to lock up, Mr Cramp.'

'It's Crump,' the old man said sourly. 'And the computers can't stay here, the room isn't secure!' he called after the disappearing headteacher.

'No problem,' Mr Macbeth called over his shoulder. 'The room has no windows, so it's safe from outside thieves. You can get a new lock fitted on the door. Goodnight, Mr Crimp.'

As we followed the Head down the corridor towards the darkening evening I could have sworn I heard Grumpy say, 'I'll get him, if it's the last thing I do, I'll get him.'

Chapter 3

'You're late,' Gran said as I walked in the front door.

'Detention,' I said.

'Hah! Is that all? When I were a lass you were lucky if you weren't strung up from the ceiling by your thumbs.'

I dropped my school bag on the floor and Baby Spark had fun pulling the books out and testing their flavours. The rest of the family had eaten tea and were watching television or doing homework. Susie, my twin sister, was trying to catch Boozle the dog's fleas while Sally was giving Sam a lecture on why he should not cut his toenails in the bath.

Dad pushed the local newspaper at me. 'Seen this?' he asked.

Duckpool Daily

CHEAP AT 30p

HEAD'S HIGH HOPES

Duckpool School's surprise new headmaster, Mr Macbeth (22), said today that Duckpool School is set to break all records in next week's tests. Last year the school was eleventh in the top ten. 'This year we'll be numero uno!' the top teacher grinned. 'I have a dream.'

Mr Macbeth was asked about the last headteacher, Mr Rodney Ramsbottom (64), who has disappeared suddenly. The new head cleverly changed the subject and said, 'I buy my stylish frog socks from a special knitwear factory in the Sahara Desert.'

It is understood that Mr Macbeth's hopes of SAT success rest on a new delivery of computers to the school. 'The delivery is a secret,' he said. 'After all, we don't want people breaking in to the school to steal them, do we? Please don't mention the new computers,' he whispered to our reporter.

I followed Gran into the kitchen. 'It's funny, but Mr Crump the caretaker said that about hanging pupils by the thumbs. You must have gone to the same school!'

Gran stirred a pan of stew and started to serve it for me. 'We did. We both went to Duckpool School. Young Cedric Crump was always in trouble. A right little tearaway! Hah! You should have heard the noises that lad could make when he was wearing a gas mask!'

'Grumpy *Crump*?' I gasped.

'Sexy Cedric, we girls called him,' Gran chuckled.

'Old Crumple-features!'

She looked at me sharply. 'We haven't always been old and wrinkly, you know. When I were a lass I climbed to the top of Mount Everest one morning and got back in time for me tea.'

'You're lying, Gran.'

'Just a little bit,' she sniffed and served the stew. 'Here's next-door's cat,' she said poking at the meat. 'I caught it digging up me carrots so I popped it in a casserole for tea. Minced Moggy. Mind you don't get a claw stuck in your throat.'

It tasted all right to me and I didn't believe her anyway. 'So what have you been up to?' she asked as she took the pepper-pot and began to top it up with salt.

'Helping the new head teacher to set up the school computers. We're on the Internet,' I said.

'Your dad's connected to that Internetty thing in his room, isn't he?'

'That's right. How did you know?'

'I sometimes have a little play when everyone's out at work and I get bored. I send those e-mail thingies to some very nice people in Mexico. This cat stew's made from a recipe I found on the Internetty.'

'You can use the Internet?' I asked.

She waved the pepper-pot at me. 'I may be old but I'm not stupid.'

'So why are you putting salt in the pepper-pot?'

'Oh, ginger snaps,' she mumbled. 'What a waste.'

'What's a waste?' Sam asked, coming in to the kitchen.

'I've put salt in the pepper and I've wasted the salt and I've wasted the pepper,' she moaned.

'Separate them,' Sam shrugged.

'What? One grain at a time?' Gran asked. 'Me eyes aren't that good.'

'No! It's a science experiment we did last year at school when we studied electricity. It's in my old exercise book! I'll get it.'

My brain was ticking loud enough to wake Spike the hamster. I had a wonderful idea. Sam's a year older than me. If he did electricity last year then I could copy all his homework for the rest of this term!

He threw the book on the kitchen table and opened it . . .

SEPARATE SALT AND PEPPER
USING STATIC ELECTRICITY

What we used
Salt, pepper, a plastic pen, a piece of woollen cloth.

What we did:
1. We sprinkled salt and pepper onto a plate (Forgot to mention the plate in the 'What we used' bit. Sorry.)
2. We rubbed the pen really hard with the wool.
3. We held the pen close to the plate but not too close.

What happened:
The pepper jumped up onto the pen. The salt stayed on the plate.
(And something else happened: everyone started to sneeze. But I don't suppose you want me to mention that, do you?)

Can I explain this?
Rubbing the pen charges it with STATIC ELECTRICITY. This attracts things. The salt and pepper are both attracted by the pen, but the pepper is lighter so it rises up first.

Any other comments?
Yeah! Why on earth would anyone want to separate salt and pepper?

'Now you know the answer,' Gran said. 'When I were a lass we never learned useful things like that at school. We learned how to knit gobstopper covers – but my gobstoppers never lasted long enough to need covering.'

While she played happily with a pen, sorting the salt from the pepper, I told Sam about the new computers and about my great plan. 'I think we should start a computer club for after school.'

'Know anyone who'd want to join?' he asked.

'A few. Myrtle Brick is always asking questions, Elvis Smith likes games and you're keen too.'

'We'll see the new Head tomorrow morning,' Sam said and slapped his hand on the table. This blew a cloud of pepper into Gran's face. She sneezed. The sneeze blew the salt on to the floor.

'Ginger snaps!' she wailed as we ran out of the room. The television screen flashed and a worried announcer's face appeared.

> A FAMILY IN SHAVE CLOSE, DUCKPOOL, HAVE
> INFORMED POLICE THAT THEIR GINGER CAT
> HAS GONE MISSING. THE CAT, WHICH ANSWERS
> TO THE NAME OF 'SOOTY', WAS LAST SEEN
> DIGGING CARROTS UP IN A NEIGHBOUR'S
> GARDEN. POLICE FEAR THE ANIMAL MAY
> ALREADY BE DEAD AND IN A CASSEROLE.
> THE FAMILY ARE HAVING KITTENS.
> ANYONE WITH ANY INFORMATION IS ASKED
> TO CONTACT DUCKPOOL POLICE WHEN
> THE STATION REOPENS NEXT WEEK AFTER
> IT'S BEEN DECORATED.

Everyone turned to the kitchen and called with one voice, 'Gran!'

She came to the door and glared at us. 'Oh, all right. I'll let it out of the garden shed.'

Chapter 4

I should have guessed it was going to be a funny sort of day when I arrived at the school next morning. A woman stopped me at the school gate. She looked like a 22-year-old disguised as a 92-year-old. Her ragged shawl hid her face – only a sharp nose poked out and her faded dress was tattered. 'Buy some lucky heather from a poor and sick old lady,' she said.

Sam stopped and stared. 'You've got a basketful,' he said.

'I have,' she said in a creaking voice.

'Well, if you've got *all* that heather, and if you're *still* poor and sick, it can't be very lucky,' he said and we walked into the school.

I could have sworn I heard her mutter, 'I hate smart brats like that.' We marched down the corridor to the headteacher's room.

We should have knocked at Mr Macbeth's door. But we didn't. We just walked straight in and saw him take something from his drawer and stuff it into his pocket. He looked up sharply. His face changed from shock to fear and back to shock. Then, like a light switch he turned on his grin. 'Simon!' he said 'What can I do for you?'

And I told him about our idea of a computer club. By the time we'd finished, Mr Macbeth was grinning at us till his teeth shone white in the morning light. 'You can start tonight. You have my full support. I will announce it in assembly.' He patted my head then wiped his hand on his black silk handkerchief. 'We can call it The Internet Club.'

'Knowing the others we'd be better calling it the Inter*nuts* Club,' I suggested.

'I like it! I can see you're like me, Simon. You have a dream!'

'No . . . but I had a nightmare last night,' I sighed. I'd dreamed Miss Trout sat down in her chair and Elvis Smith plugged it into the electric socket. It was very messy.

Mr Crump watched us enter the school hall. 'Try not to walk on my floors,' he groaned. 'I spent hours last night polishing them! Hours I spent!' He didn't look a 'Sexy Cedric' to me.

The teachers lined up on the platform looking as cheerful as if their budgie had just died. Everyone stared up at Mr Macbeth in his shining suit. He ran a hand through his permed hair. I waited for him to announce the Internuts Club, but instead he looked at us with sad shocked eyes. 'This morning, I have some serious and dreadfully sad news . . .' Even the teachers seemed to wake up and listen.

'When I arrived in my office this morning I found something that shocked me,' Mr Macbeth said.

Elvis nudged me and whispered, 'I bet Grumpy had cleaned the room for a change!'

Mr Macbeth looked round very slowly and glared at us. Elvis tried to shrink his head into his shoulders but he looked like a stuck tortoise. I didn't feel like laughing.

'I came to this school with a dream. I want this to be the best school in the town. And you have let me down.' The hall was silent. No one was shuffling or coughing. 'Someone has been into my office and stolen from my desk.'

You could hear a gasp from the children and the crash as the teachers' jaws hit the floor.

No one had ever stolen anything at Duckpool School before. Well, not from the Head's office. 'I am going to find out who the thief is,' Mr Macbeth went on. 'And they are going to be punished.'

We looked at one other and tried to see who looked guilty. The trouble was, we all looked guilty. Even the teachers looked guilty. Miss Trout leaned forward and said, 'Mr Macbeth, I'm sure all the children want to help. But could you tell us what was taken?'

'Sweets for the tuck shop.'

Everyone relaxed a bit. Taking sweets wasn't that serious, was it?

'It may be sweets this time but who knows what the thief will take next time. Will it be the new computers? Or the money to pay for the computers, secretly hidden in my office safe?' he carried on.

'Why's he got computers in his office safe?' Elvis frowned.

'The *money* for the computers is what's in the safe.'

Elvis wiped his nose on his sleeve.

'Does anyone have any information that might help?' Mr Macbeth asked in a funereal voice.

I felt my hand rise into the air. 'Mr Macbeth,' I said, 'there was a strange woman hanging around the school gates this morning.'

'Thank you, Simon,' he said but his eyes were staring and glinting like a robot. 'I don't think a strange woman would be interested in our sweets or know they were there. I suspect the culprit is nearer. I suspect the culprit is in this very hall.' He walked slowly down the steps from the stage and went to the back of the hall. 'Dismiss!'

As we walked out in silence, he stood and watched each of us. His eyes burning into the backs of our necks. It was only when we reached the classroom that I realized that he had forgotten to mention the computer club. I didn't want to go and remind him so I explained the club to Miss Trout. She didn't really understand what I was on about – nothing new there.

'I'll have a word with Mr Macbeth once you've started work,' she said. 'Now let's get on with this work on electricity.'

'Why?' Myrtle asked, as alert as ever.

'Today you are going to build a circuit.'

'Can't we build a monster?' Elvis asked.

'We don't need to, we've got Crumpy,' I muttered.

'Myrtle, hand out the worksheets, please.'

'Why?'

Miss Trout sighed and wandered out of the room. The worksheet didn't look very exciting but they never do. I didn't know, of course, that this electric stuff was going to save our lives and our school.

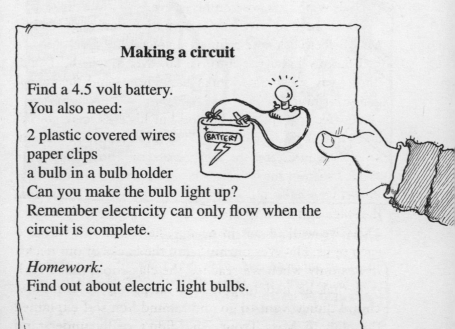

Making a circuit

Find a 4.5 volt battery.
You also need:

2 plastic covered wires
paper clips
a bulb in a bulb holder
Can you make the bulb light up?
Remember electricity can only flow when the circuit is complete.

Homework:
Find out about electric light bulbs.

'What shall we do now?' Elvis asked when we finished.

The classroom door crashed open as Grumpy Crumpy came in carrying a box. He was muttering to himself. Either that or he has an imaginary friend that he chats to.

'Accusing me? Me? The nerve of the man. Who does he think he is? Been here two minutes. Young upstart,' he grumbled. 'Tell Miss Trout I've brought the new batteries and bulb,' he said to no one in particular.

Miss Trout came back in, followed by a kid with a broken ankle and a message. I've never worked out why teachers get the children who are injured to take messages round the school. It must take them hours.

Miss Trout read out the message,

TONIGHT WILL BE THE FIRST MEETING OF THE NEW COMPUTER CLUB. ANYONE WHO IS INTERESTED MUST MEET IN THE COMPUTER ROOM AFTER SCHOOL.

I looked at Elvis and Myrtle and winked.

'That's all I need – loads of kids cluttering up the school when I'm trying to clean. Kids. Do nothing but make a mess. Kids, ' Grumpy grumped.

'Mr Macbeth's looking for you, Mr Crump,' Miss Trout said.

'Oh great. That's all I need. I say, that's all I need,' he complained as he dragged himself out of the room.

'Mr Crumb, we need to talk,' Mr Macbeth's voice sliced through the air.

'The name's Crump, I say. Crump! I've told you once I don't know nothing about no theft. I was out all evening.'

Elvis and I looked at each other with open mouths. 'Mr Macbeth thinks the thief is . . . Grumpy!'

Chapter 5

The Internuts Club was a great success. That first night we had four members. Sam and me, Elvis and Myrtle. What d'you mean, 'That's not many'? Even the Famous Five only had one more – and one of them was a dog, I think! If we let Spike the Hamster into the Internuts we could call ourselves the Famouser Five!

The little room with the computers had been cleared but it still smelled of cleaning fluid and stale mops. There was a single, feeble light bulb in the ceiling and no windows to the outside. At least the computers were new and working.

'Homework first then we can surf the net,' I said.

'We'll get wet,' Elvis said.

'No, Elvis,' Sam sighed. 'Surfing the net means exploring the Internet.'

'Why?' Myrtle said.

'Yeah,' Elvis agreed. '*Why* didn't you say so in the first place.'

I shrugged and typed in a search for 'electric' and 'bulbs'. There was so much we were each able to write something different.

I wrote . . .

Electric lights by Simon Spark

In 1860 a man called Joseph Swan built the first lightbulb. He passed electricity through a filament inside a glass bowl. All the air had been sucked out of the bowl to make a vacuum. The filament glowed and gave off a light. Joseph lived in a sunny land... (oops, sorry, I mean he lived in an English town called Sunderland). He was very bright. Sadly his electric light wasn't so bright.

ELEKTRIC LIGHTS by ELVIS SMITH

This American geezer called Thomas Edison took Joe Swan's idea and made it better and ~~brighterer~~ brighter. It took him twenty years! When he finally cracked it he must have been one happy man. He found the best filaments were made from bamboo ~~the~~ Sticks. Teechers canes were also made from bamboo Sticks.

Queshtun: Did Edison's canes hurt you?

Answer: No, cos they were very light.

(This is a JOKE Miss Trout)

Electric lights by Myrtle Brick.

Edison and Swan's little electric light bulbs were fiddly and hard to make. But in the 1860's they could make dirty great electric arc lamps. These had the power of 38 million candles so they'd blind you if you tried to use them to read in bed. They were great for lighthouses though. An English lighthouse in Dungeness used an electric light in 1862. I wish I lived in a lighthouse, but our house is dead heavy.

Love, Myrtle

XXX

'We'll get top marks in the SATs with this sort of work,' I said excitedly.

Elvis leaned forward and whispered, 'We'll get top marks anyway.'

We all leaned forward and the green glow from the computer screen made us look like aliens. 'How do you know?'

'My brother, Elton, says he heard the teachers talking about that letter from the council. You know, the one you nicked from Miss Trout's desk, Sparky.'

'The one that told teachers not to cheat?' I asked.

'Yeah. Well, the teachers reckon Mr Macbeth *wants* them to use all those top tips in the letter. He wants us to come top of the league!'

'Why?' Myrtle asked, as usual.

'I don't know, Myrtle. Elton said the teachers said something about him being very ambitious. If he makes this the best school in the county then they'll give him a bigger school next time – more money!'

'Why?'

'Bigger Jaguar car, I expect,' Elvis shrugged. None of us felt very happy about cheating. Old Mr Ramsbottom was a bit boring but he always told us, 'Cheats never beats.' We never even cheated in the school football matches – which is why we lost most games 10–0 at least.

'Wonder what happened to old Rams-bum?' I murmured.

'Look on the Internet for news,' Sam said. 'It's more up to date than the newspapers.'

I typed in a search for 'Ramsbottom' and 'Duckpool'. There were half a dozen articles but the latest one was dated that afternoon. I brought it up on the screen.

Missing head

Police are still puzzled by the disappearance of Mr Rodney Ramsbottom. The headteacher of the worst school in Duckpool went missing a week ago. Detective Constable Laurence Olivier Elloe said today that Mr Ramsbottom was last seen buying lucky heather from a mysterious woman outside his local fish shop. 'The heather wasn't all that lucky,' DC Elloe said.

 'A fast car was heard driving off shortly after. We are afraid that Mr Ramsbottom may have had his chips.'

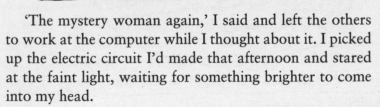

'The mystery woman again,' I said and left the others to work at the computer while I thought about it. I picked up the electric circuit I'd made that afternoon and stared at the faint light, waiting for something brighter to come into my head.

The door swung open. 'You kids got nothing better to do than hang around school? When I were a lad I was out of here like a shot, playing football on the beach till the tide came in over our heads! Over our heads, I say.'

'It's dark at four o'clock now, Mister Crump,' I reminded him.

'So use a torch,' he said. He picked up the light bulb circuit I'd built and sniffed. 'This would do. Mind, you want to put a switch in that.'

'Why?' Myrtle asked.

'Otherwise the bulb will be on all the time. Wear the battery out in no time. Wear it clean out.'

'How do we make a switch?' I asked.

'Two drawing pins, a paper clip and a bit of balsa wood should do it,' he explained. 'Give me that scrap of paper and I'll draw it for you.'

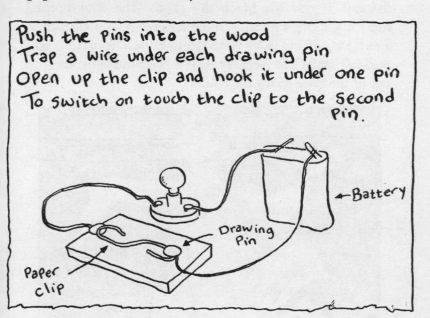

Push the pins into the wood
Trap a wire under each drawing pin
Open up the clip and hook it under one pin
To switch on touch the clip to the second pin.

Battery

Drawing Pin

Paper clip

A couple of inutes later he'd put a switch into my circuit. It was really neat. 'That's brilliant, Mr Crump!' Elvis said.

The old man nodded. 'Little trick I learned in the SAS.'

'You were in the SAS?' I gasped.

'Certainly. I was a founder member.'

'The Special Air Services?'

'Nah! The Southwold Aero-modellers' Society. I've still got the club badge on my anorak,' he said proudly. 'Now it's five o'clock. I'm off home for my tea. I want you out so I can lock up. I say, I want to lock up!'

We switched the computer off, packed our homework into our bags and followed him into the corridor. He carefully locked the door behind us and walked down the corridor switching lights off. There was one light left on at the end. It was Mr Macbeth's room. The door opened suddenly, I saw a gleam of blue and white as a woman in a nurse's uniform came out. The light was behind her so I couldn't make out her face. She turned suddenly and ran out of the door at the far end.

'What're you up to?' Grumpy cried. 'I say, what're you up to?' But the woman was gone into the cold night and the yard was empty except for a whirl of dead leaves and deader crisp packets.

Mr Crump turned back to the headteacher's room and reached for the light switch. Suddenly he cried, 'Oh, my Gawd! I said ohhhh, my Gawwwwd!'

Chapter 6

We Internuts slipped our heads under Mr Crump's arms as he held on to the door frame for support. The head-teacher's room was empty. We followed his gaze across to the far wall. A heavy metal door to the headteacher's safe stood wide open.

Elvis shot past the caretaker. 'Nobody touch a thing. The police will want to take fingerprints!'

'No they won't,' the caretaker said.

'Why?' Myrtle asked.

'Because the safe's still full of money. We disturbed her before she could nick it.'

But, when Grumpy phoned Mr Macbeth and he arrived with a roar of his red Jag, he had a different story. He checked the money, sat back in his chair and put his feet on the desk while we stood in front of him like crooks. I noticed his black socks had gold aeroplanes on them this evening.

'We saved your money,' Elvis said. 'We caught the woman red-footed.'

Mr Macbeth's smile was dazzling as ever. 'Or maybe the woman saved the money. Maybe someone else had opened the safe and was about to take the cash when the school nurse walked in.'

'But who?' I asked.

Mr Macbeth gave a sort of shrug with his eyebrows. 'Someone in the school already.'

'No one in the Internuts,' Sam said quickly. 'No one left the computer room.'

The headteacher spread his hands. 'So, who else?' he asked and looked at Mr Crump.

The old man turned bright red then went deathly pale. He said nothing but turned and walked out of the school. 'Thank you, Internuts,' Mr Macbeth said. 'You'd better get home. I'll lock up.'

It was a miserable and quiet trudge home through the cold and deserted streets. Gran saw how unhappy Sam and I were. She sat us at the kitchen table and asked, 'You look like you've lost a fiver and found a penny. What's up?'

Sam and I told the story. Gran listened carefully and her wrinkled face was creased in a deep frown. She said nothing that night.

But, next morning, I noticed Gran wasn't herself. Well, she doesn't usually cook bacon and custard for breakfast. I gave mine to Boozle, the dog, but even he refused to eat it.

'We might be late home tonight, Gran,' I said.

Sam tried to get through to her. 'Gran, Simon and I will be staying for computer club at school tonight.'

'I've been thinking,' she said.

'Oh, no!' we cried. When Gran thinks it always means trouble. Sam raced out of the room and Boozle dived for the cat flap. And got stuck. Again.

'I've been thinking about poor Cedric. It sounds to me like he could be in serious trouble,' she said.

'He certainly looked worried last night,' I said.

'I remember seeing him for the first time. I was standing in the playground. The autumn sun was glinting off the headteacher's bald spot and blinding the boys playing football. This tall skinny kid wandered past me. He wasn't like the other lads.'

'Why not?' I asked.

'He was *clean*. Up until then I thought all boys were born with mud-covered, blood-stained knees and dripping noses. Cedric was different,' she sighed.

'Come on, Simon, or we'll be late,' Sam called from the hall.

'Tell Cedric that I'll bring the burglar alarm in at the end of school,' Gran said.

'The burglar alarm. What burglar alarm?' I asked.

'The one I'm going to build. The one that will catch the thief and clear Cedric's name,' she said showing me the page from one of the ancient magazines she kept in the attic.

Top Tips for the Housewife Number 102

Worried about home security? Scared of who might come in and steal your wireless set or the savings in your tea caddy? Here's the answer. Keep your family safe and save money. Build your own burglar alarm. Here are simple step-by-step instructions for the simple housewife.

Step 1. Find all the equipment. You may have to go to the shops and buy some of it. A piece of card (about 15cm by 8cm), a 4.5 volt battery, some wires, sticky tape, a small buzzer, tin foil, and paper clips.
Step 2. Fold the card in half and wrap a piece of foil around each half.
Step 3. Tape a wire to each piece of foil. Does your piece of card look like this?
Step 4. Connect the other ends of the wires like this.

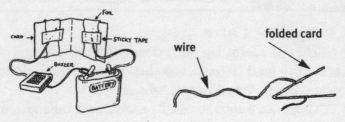

Step 5. Put the card under a rug near the door. When the burglar walks in they will stand on the rug and the buzzer will sound.

I passed Crumpy on my way into school and told him about Gran's burglar alarm.

'No need, lad. I say, no need. Got my own plan. Got to look after yourself in this world, my lad,' he grumped. 'But I'm grateful to Gertie, tell her.' He added quietly, 'It would be nice to see Gorgeous Gertie again.'

Some days nothing much happens in school. No one fell off their chair. No one threw up. No one had a fight. It was a very dull day. The only thing we could do was work.

At the end of the day, the Internuts met in the computer room. The room still smelled. I looked at Elvis and sniffed. It was after-shave.

'How long have you been shaving, Elvis?' I asked.

'It's not me. It's Grumpy over there,' he answered.

Before the caretaker could say anything Gran walked in carrying a box. Grumpy leapt to his feet. I didn't know he could move that fast.

'Evening, Cedric. I've brought you a burglar alarm,' she said.

'Evening, Gertrude.' He placed a pair of spectacles on the end of his nose and examined the alarm carefully. 'Don't think I'm not grateful. I say, don't think that. But there was no need. Built one meself. I say, I've *built* one. Would you care to do me the honour of inspecting it?' He led Gran out of the room and towards Mr Macbeth's office. We followed them. Wouldn't you?

'Tell me it's not the old method, Cedric?' Gran said.

'Always worked in my day,' he said confidently. 'Never failed.'

'No Cedric, it never worked.'

The sound of a bucket crashing to the floor was followed by a woman's scream.

'It's worked,' Grumpy shouted. 'My burglar alarm worked.'

We ran to the office just in time to see a woman dressed

49

as a cowgirl running for the door. She was covered in flour. The wide hat and the flour on her face made it hard to recognize her. Grumpy looked at me and frowned. 'Strange,' he said. 'There's no line-dancing class tonight.'

Chapter 7

Of course Grumpy's burglar alarm had been a bucket of flour over the door. When the mystery woman opened the door the bucket fell on her head. I left Gran and Mr Crump to vacuum up the flour. Gran was explaining, 'With my alarm you'll know when the burglar's in the room, but the burglar won't know you know? You know what I mean?'

'I know.'

'So, let's get it set up,' she said. 'I doubt if she'll come back tonight.'

While they did that the Internuts searched the Internet. First we looked for the latest news on Mr Ramsbottom. All it said was:

MISSING HEAD TEACHER, RODNEY RAMSBOTTOM, IS STILL MISSING. HE DISAPPEARED FROM DUCKPOOL FISH SHOP AND A FAST CAR WAS HEARD DRIVING AWAY. TODAY DETECTIVE CONSTABLE LAURENCE OLIVIER ELLOE REVEALED THAT A NEW CLUE HAD BEEN FOUND. "TYRE TRACKS FROM THE CAR HAVE BEEN FOUND ON THE CORPSE OF AN UNFORTUNATE HEDGEHOG THAT GOT IN THE WAY...

'I wish I was a detective,' Elvis said. 'I'd find old Rams-bum and I'd solve the mystery of the school burglar.'

'Why?' Myrtle asked.

'Get me name in the papers and even me picture!' Elvis sniffed. Police use sniffer dogs but I didn't think they'd want a sniffy boy.

'Maybe we *could* be detectives!' Sam said. 'This room is the perfect hiding-place. We could stay in here when the school closes. The burglar alarm would tell us when someone enters Mr Macbeth's room . . .'

'No-o!' Elvis moaned. 'I'm not getting b-bashed by some b-big b-bad b-bruising b-burglar.'

'I agree,' I said. It wasn't often I agreed with Elvis but this was one time when he was right. I'm not a coward. I just don't like getting hurt.

'Fine,' Sam said. 'We wait for the burglar alarm to go off then we signal to someone outside. Myrtle can wait outside.'

'Why?'

'Because you're a fast runner. You can run and fetch the police!' Sam cried.

'Hang on,' I said. 'There's no window in this room. How do we wave to Myrtle through a brick wall?'

'We hide Myrtle in the gym. She can get to any door from there. Look . . .'

Sam drew a sketch of the school.

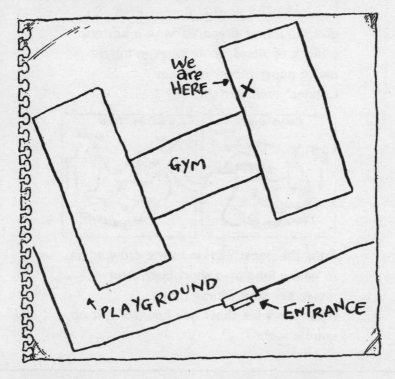

'We'll run a wire from here to Myrtle,' Sam said.

'Yeah,' Elvis nodded. 'Wire Myrtle up. When the burglar comes we switch the power on and give Myrtle a shock! Heh! Heh!'

Myrtle stuck out her bottom lip and glared at him.

'No,' Sam said. 'We connect a battery to an electric buzzer and put a switch in the circuit. When the burglar comes in the school we buzz Myrtle. It's in my latest Boy Scout magazine,' he said and pulled it out of his school bag. It looked simple enough.

Making a telegraph

Scouts have a motto, 'Be prepared'. So
you should 'be prepared' with a battery,
a block of wood, some wires, a buzzer
and a paper clip at all times.
Connect them like this

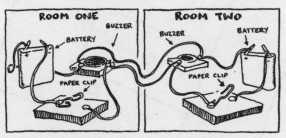

Press the paper clip on to the drawing pin
to give a long or a short buzz. And
remember your Morse Code!
(Next week we show you how to light up
your woggle!)

'What's this Morse Code? Is it what the Vikings used?'
Elvis asked.

'No, they're *Norse*. This is *Morse*,' Sam sighed. 'Mr
Morse was called Sam like all the cleverest people. He
invented this electric telegraph then he invented a way of
sending messages down the line. Three short bleeps was
the letter 'S', a short and a long is 'A' and two long bleeps
is 'M', and so on. Blip-blip-blip, blip-bleep, bleep-bleep
spells S-A-M.'

'Why didn't he just pick up a telephone?' Elvis demanded.

'Because he invented this in 1838 before telephones had been thought of. Look it up on the Internet,' Sam explained patiently.

We did and we found the code . . .

MORSE CODE

A	.—		S	...
B	—...		T	—
C	—.—.		U	..—
D	—..		V	...—
E	.		W	.——
F	..—.		X	—..—
G	——.		Y	—.——
H	....		Z	——..
I	..		1	.————
J	.———		2	..———
K	—.—		3	...——
L	.—..		4	....—
M	——		5	.....
N	—.		6	—....
O	———		7	——...
P	.——.		8	———..
Q	——.—		9	————.
R	.—.		0	—————

We also found that most people had stopped using it by 1998 because radios and telephones were much better. Still, it would do the job for us. We printed out copies so everyone could learn the code and Sam promised to make the telegraph.

When we left the Internuts' computer room we found Mr Crump bringing the burglar alarm wire to the room. 'Useful this,' he said. 'Every time someone goes in or out of Mr Macbeth's room I'll know. Thank you, Gertrude.'

'A pleasure, Cedric,' Gran replied.

They stood and looked at one another. The four Internuts looked at them.

'It's been nice seeing you again, after all these years,' the caretaker said.

'You're still as clean as ever,' Gran said.

'I pride myself on my floor polishing,' the old man said. 'You could eat your dinner off these floors. Eat your dinner!'

'Someone would have to invite me to dinner first,' Gran said.

Suddenly the door at the end of the corridor swung open with a crash. 'What's been going on here?' Mr Macbeth demanded. He strode down the corridor, his heels clicking on the glimmering floor. 'Another break-in and you let the burglar get away, eh, Mr Clump? Careless of you . . . unless you *wanted* the suspect to escape.'

The caretaker's face turned purple. 'Why would I do that? Why, I say?'

'Because you are in league with these villains. I've always suspected it,' Mr Macbeth said. 'Either that or you're just too old for the job. Have you ever thought of retiring, Mr Gamp?'

'No.'

'Then I suggest you do so,' the Head said. 'I have a dream and you aren't part of it. Retire or I call the police. You have twenty-four hours to decide. Now I will lock the school myself. Just to be on the safe side.'

Gran turned to her old friend. 'Would you like me to smack him round the ear with me handbag, Cedric?'

'Thank you, Gertrude, but it would do no good.'

'It would if I put a brick inside it,' Gran said and marched out of the doors as if she meant to go in search of one.

Mr Macbeth hurried us out. 'Glamp's days are numbered,' he muttered as I walked past him into the cold night air.

Chapter 8

By the next day the Internuts were ready for the burglar-watch. We had crisps, sandwiches and chocolate. We'd all told our parents we'd be staying at a friend's house – a friend without a telephone so they couldn't check up.

The burglar-watch was so exciting the lessons seemed to drag. But Miss Trout did give us an idea during the science lesson.

'Today's electricity lesson is going to be such fun, children.' Miss Trout said. We groaned.

She continued, 'I've got something exciting for you all to make. I made mine last night.'

'I'm not knitting a lampshade,' growled Elvis.

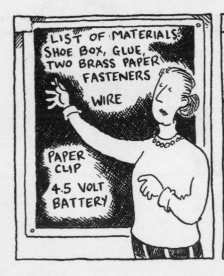

LIST OF MATERIALS:
SHOE BOX, GLUE,
TWO BRASS PAPER
FASTENERS

WIRE

PAPER
CLIP

4.5 VOLT
BATTERY

2 I TOOK THE LID OF MY SHOE BOX AND CUT A SLIT IN THE CORNERS OF ONE LONG SIDE. THIS IS THE HINGE.

3 THEN I MADE A HOLE FOR A PAPER FASTENER IN ONE CORNER OF THE LID TOP – NEAR THE HINGE – AND POPPED IT IN..

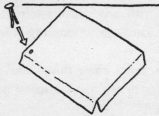

4 NEXT I GLUED THE HINGE ON TO THE SHOE BOX AND CHECKED THAT IT OPENED AND SHUT EASILY

5 THEN I MADE ANOTHER HOLE FOR A PAPER FASTENER IN THE HINGE. IT NEEDS TO BE JUST BELOW THE FIRST FASTENER

6 I TOOK MY PAPER CLIP AND SLID IT OVER THE SECOND FASTENER. WHEN I OPENED THE LID THE FIRST PAPER FASTENER TOUCHED THE PAPER CLIP. ISN'T THIS EXCITING?

7 PUT YOUR BATTERY INSIDE THE BOX. JOIN THE WIRES LIKE THIS: BATTERY TO BUZZER, BUZZER TO PAPERCLIP, PAPER FASTENER TO BATTERY

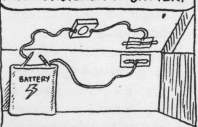

BATTERY

8 SEE, WHEN I OPEN THE LID THE BUZZER WILL SOUND. ISN'T THAT CLEVER, CHILDREN? WOULD YOU LIKE TO MAKE ONE?

BUZZZZZZZZ

ZZZZZZ

ZZZZZZ

ZZZZZZ

59

'Now you can keep all your treasures safe,' Miss Trout said.

I nudged Elvis before he started snoring. 'Elvis, I've had an idea,' I said.

'I don't think I can cope with any more excitement today,' he said. Little did we know how exciting it was going to be.

'We'll make one of those treasure chest things and get Crumpy to swap it for the box in the safe. Then if anything is stolen, it won't matter.'

'Brilliant. You are a genius,' Elvis said.

'Why?' Myrtle asked.

'Practice,' I said.

At the end of school we found Mr Crump and gave him the fake cash box. Even he seemed impressed with the idea.

'I'll wait until Macbeth goes home and then swap the boxes. When the thief comes your Gran's alarm will go off. And then we'll have them,' he grinned at me. We

walked back to the computer room as the sound of tyres screeching to a halt cut through the air.

'That sounds like a fast car,' said Elvis.

'Mr Ramsbottom was taken in a fast car,' added Sam.

We ran to the window to see what was happening. Elvis was right. It was a fast car. A police car. And inside were two fast policemen. They ran into school and a few minutes later walked out with Mr Crump – in handcuffs.

'Cor, that was fast!' said Elvis.

'How many times do I have to tell you?' Mr Crump was shouting. 'I wasn't taking anything from the safe.'

They pushed old Grumpy in the police car and drove off. The plan was not going as planned. Back in the computer room we had to think.

'It's all down to us now. We'll have to listen out for Gran's burglar alarm and then get the police,' I said.

'But we can't hear it from here,' Elvis said, splattering the wall with a mouthful of crisps.

'We'll wire the buzzer up to the Internuts' computer room,' I suggested. 'Myrtle, let's find somewhere for you to hide.'

'Why?'

'The burglar will strike tonight. We'll keep watch in the computer room to see who it is. When the burglar arrives we buzz you and you can run for help.'

I looked around the hall and found the perfect hiding-place. In the vaulting box in the hall. I ran the telegraph wires out of the computer room, along the wall and into the box. Myrtle climbed into the box and I handed her some crisps and chocolate and put the top of the box back on.

'Don't make any noise, Myrtle,' I said through the hand-hold in the side.

'Why?' she asked.

'In case the burglar hears you.'

'How's she going to eat the crisps quietly?' Sam asked.

'Suck 'em.'

The three of us squeezed into the computer room and waited. All the equipment was working. The burglar alarm. The telegraph. Nothing could go wrong. We were going to catch the thief red-handed.

The whole school was quiet. Inside the room the only sound we could hear was Elvis's stomach rumbling. Then we heard footsteps in the corridor, coming slowly towards Mr Macbeth's office. This was it. We were going to catch the burglar. We were going to be heroes. And then the footsteps reached our door and stopped . . . we heard a click. We were locked in the computer room.

Chapter 9

'Trapped!' Elvis groaned.

'Doomed!' Sam moaned.

'No one knows we're here!' the snivelling Smith snuffled.

'We could starve to death. They could open this cupboard in a year's time and find three skeletons,' my brother breathed.

'Oh, stop whinging and send a signal to Myrtle,' I snapped. 'That's what she's there for.'

'I can't,' Sam said. 'Whoever walked down the corridor kicked the wire. There's just a little showing under the door.'

'So add some more wire and connect it to the telegraph. Where's the wire?'

'In the classroom.'

'Go and get it.'

'I can't.'

'Why not?'

'Cos we're locked in here.'

'I forgot.'

We sank on to the chairs in gloom.

'Trapped,' Elvis said. 'I told you so.'

'Doomed. I told you so.' Sam added.

'Not while we're on the Internet,' I said. 'First I'll send an e-mail message to our house. With any luck someone will check the e-mails tonight and rescue us.'

'Or check it in a year's time and find our skeletons,' Elvis sighed.

I ignored him and sent off a quick message.

I was pleased with the message. 'That will make sure we're safe. Now we just need to contact Myrtle to try and

TO: THE SPARK FAMILY
FROM: SIMON SPARK AND SAM
        SPARK AND ELVIS SMITH
SUBJECT: HELP!
MESSAGE: WE HAVE BEEN LOCKED
IN DUCKPOOL SCHOOL COMPUTER
ROOM BY A BURGLAR. PLEASE
SEND POLICE AT ONCE.
        SIMON.
P.S. ELVIS SAYS CAN YOU
BRING A BAG OF CHIPS
WITH YOU.

make sure the thief doesn't get away. What we need is something to link the wire with the telegraph. We need a conductor.'

And I waited.

I waited for Elvis to say, 'My auntie used to be a bus conductor. Shame she's not here.'

He didn't say that. I was amazed and thrilled. Sometimes life is full of pleasant surprises. I typed 'conductor' into the 'Search' box on the computer screen.

'"A conductor is any material that lets heat or electricity pass through it,"' I said, reading the screen. '"Metals are good conductors and so is graphite." Graphite? Where do you get graphite?' I typed the word into the computer.

'"Graphite – a soft black mineral, made of carbon, and used as the 'lead' in pencils!"' I turned to the other two! 'A lead pencil will make the connection. The graphite in the pencil's a good conductor.'

You can try this yourself. Do experiment 4 again – 'Making A Circuit'. Take a wire off the battery and put one end of the pencil on the battery terminal, the other on the wire. Look, this is what I mean . . .

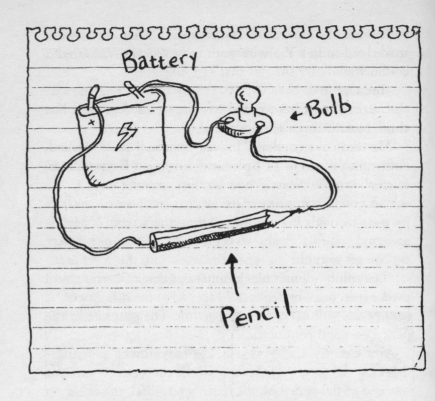

Anyway, I told the others that the 'lead' in a pencil was a good conductor.

'My uncle used to be a good conductor,' Elvis said. 'He used to punch tickets. One day he punched the driver on the nose and he got the sack.'

Sometimes life can be cruel. I decided to ignore Elvis. I passed my best art pencil to Sam and told him to hold one end to the bare wire and one to the telegraph. I slowly tapped out the message. 'M-y-r-t-l-e g-o f-o-r c-o-p-s.'

I waited a minute and the reply began to come through. 'Blip-bleep-bleep. W!' I told the others. 'Blip-blip-blip-blip. H! And Bleep-blip-bleep. K?'

'W – H – K?' Sam asked. 'What does "whuk" mean?'

'I think she missed the last bleep off. That would have made the K into a Y. She meant to say W – H – Y. "Why?"'

'So why *didn't* she put that last bleep in?'

'Because she's been cut off. I think the school's so quiet the burglar must have heard her buzzer and cut her off. I think Myrtle's been got, lads. She could be in real trouble.'

We went silent and gloomy for a while. Then Elvis said, softly, 'I saw this in a film once. Three people locked in a bank vault. They ran out of air. They stuffycated! That's what's going to happen to us!'

It was getting hot in there. The air was nearly as thick as Elvis.

'We have to breathe less,' I said.

'Let's all hold out breaths and save air,' Sam suggested.

We held our breaths . . .

'It isn't going to work!' Elvis panted . . . and used up ten minutes of air – *my* air. 'I reckon we have just twenty minutes to live!'

Chapter 10

'I'm not going to sit here and just sweat to death. There must be something we can do,' I said.

'When they find us, I'll just be a big puddle of sweat on the floor,' moaned Elvis.

I tried to ignore him. 'We need more air. The only thing we've got in here is a load of old mops and a tap.'

'And the computer,' Sam reminded me. 'Maybe the answer is there!'

I typed air and water into the computer search and we waited.

'If that computer tells us how to make air from water then I'm a squirrel,' Elvis said.

The computer screen flickered.

IS THERE ANY EQUIPMENT I NEED TO TAKE?

I ALWAYS TAKE TWO PENCILS SHARPENED AT BOTH ENDS, A PIECE OF PAPER, A GLASS JAR, SOME WIRE AND A 4.5 VOLT BATTERY!

THEN YOU CAN MAKE YOUR OWN OXYGEN!

AMAZING!

HERE'S WHAT YOU DO, EGBERT:
① PUT SOME WATER INTO A JAR AND PLACE A PIECE OF PAPER ON TOP.

② STICK THE PENCILS THROUGH THE PAPER INTO THE WATER...

③ PUT A LOOP OF WIRE OVER THE TOP OF EACH PENCIL. CONNECT THE OTHER ENDS OF THE WIRE TO THE BATTERY

YOU WILL SEE BUBBLES AROUND THE PENCIL TIPS. THESE ARE HYDROGEN AND OXYGEN

Sam and I grabbed all the equipment and set up the experiment. Elvis sat in the corner and looked miserable.

'I'm hungry,' said Elvis.

'Can't you remember where you hid your nuts, *squirrel*?' Sam replied.

'You be nice to me or . . . or I'll take my shoes off!' he threatened.

'Oh no, not the socks!' I said.

'No sense of humour, these squirrels,' Sam whispered.

'I'm cold,' Elvis moaned. 'It's draughty in here.'

He was right. There was a breeze coming from under the door. Someone must have opened the school doors. That fresh air could also save us!

'Myrtle must have got out. She's come to rescue us,' I said.

I raised my hand to hammer on the door. Sam grabbed my arm. 'What if it isn't Myrtle?' he said. 'What if it's the burglar?'

'What if it's someone with my chips?' Elvis added.

'Shhhh, listen,' I whispered.

I recognized the man's voice and I'd heard the woman's voice too . . . selling me lucky heather. But why was he in school this late and talking to the mystery woman? It didn't make sense.

'Put the money back,' he said. 'If we take it then our plan will be ruined.'

'But I need to buy some new clothes,' she said.

'You bought some this week,' he said.

'I bought that nurse's uniform as one of my disguises,' she told him.

It couldn't be. Could it?

'Look,' the man said. 'Crimp is in the police station. If we take the money now then even the Duckpool police will work out that he isn't the thief.'

'Good point.' Two sets of footsteps marched down the corridor towards Mr Macbeth's room. The burglar alarm flashed.

'It's working, look, it's working!' Elvis shouted.

'What was that noise?' the man's voice asked.

Sam and I glared at Elvis. We froze and held our breath.

'You must be hearing things. Come on, let's get out of here,' the woman said.

Then we heard their footsteps. They were coming closer and closer to the computer room. This was it. The thief had come to get us. The lock snapped open. We watched the door handle turn. We were doomed.

CREEAK...

Chapter 11

The lock clicked. The door handle turned. The door swung open. And Mr Macbeth looked into the room. 'Good evening, Internuts,' he said and his teeth glittered green in the reflected light of the computer screen. 'How much do you know?'

'Nothing,' I said.

'Nothing,' Sam said.

'Everything!' Elvis squawked. 'That woman is the burglar and she's a friend of yours! You've been helping her to rob Duckpool School.'

The woman had eyes as hard as the rounders' bat Mr Macbeth held in his hand. Her face was pointy – pointy nose, pointy chin and spiky hair. She looked as if she could

tear open a polar bear with her long, sharp, finger-nails.

'Almost right, Elvis. But this woman is in fact my wife,' our headteacher said.

'We're going to the police to get Mr Crump set free, and to have you arrested,' I said.

'You can't do that from inside a locked cupboard,' Mr Macbeth grinned nastily. 'If I block off the bottom of the door you will suffocate before they find you in the morning. Of course, I will make sure the useless old caretaker gets the blame for that too. We'll say he locked you in and left you before he was arrested.'

'No you won't,' said a quiet voice from the far end of the corridor. We swung round. Gran stood there, feet slightly apart, handbag swinging slowly from her arm. Then she moved. A steady, menacing plod up the gleaming corridor floor. The street lights behind made a halo of her white hair.

Mrs Macbeth gave a low hiss and turned to face Gran. 'Another old loony to join Crump in the clink,' she said.

Gran's mouth was hard and her lips pale. 'I've got a brick in this handbag.'

'What?' gasped the Macbeths. They backed away from her until they were up against the wall.

'I've got a brick in here . . . and it's loaded. One false move from you rattlesnakes and I'll brick you till you beg for mercy. Drop your weapon!' she ordered. Mr Macbeth let the rounders' bat clatter to the floor. 'Now get in that room,' she said.

We all crowded into the computer room while Sam ran to call the police. It was a tight fit in the room and the smell of Mrs Macbeth's perfume was a bit sickening – but it was better than Elvis's socks. Sam winked at Gran, 'You got the e-mail then?'

'I did.'

'Why didn't you just call the police?' I asked.

'Because a Gran's gotta do what a Gran's gotta do,' she said.

'I have a dream, you know. We were just trying to make Duckpool School the best in the country,' Mr Macbeth said and his voice was a whine now.

'By robbing it?' I laughed.

'No, by getting the old man the sack. I wanted my wife to get his job, you see. She's an artist – a decorator. She'd turn this crumbling mess into a palace of learning! We only wanted what's best for the children,' Mr Macbeth said and there was a sob in his voice.

'You're a liar,' Gran said.

'Prove it,' Mrs Macbeth sneered.

Gran gave a slow smile and nodded. 'I will.'

SHE PICKED UP OUR CIRCUIT WITH THE BATTERY, THE LIGHT AND THE PENCIL

SHE FILLED A JAM JAR WITH WATER

SHE TOOK A SALT CELLAR AND TEASPOON FROM HER HANDBAG AND STIRRED FOUR TEASPOONS OF SALT INTO THE JAR

SHE DIPPED THE TWO ENDS OF THE WIRE INTO THE SALT WATER AND THE BULB GLOWED...

'Salt is sodium chloride,' she told us. 'And sodium is a metal. Metal is a good conductor.'

Elvis opened his mouth. Gran turned on him sharply. 'And if you say a word about your uncle being a conductor you'll get a taste of my brick, young Elvis Smith.' He closed his mouth.

'What's this got to do with us?' Mr Macbeth said.

'Sweat is salty water,' Gran said. 'When you tell a lie then the palms of your hands sweat. I will tape these wires to the palm of your hand and ask you some questions. When you lie, your palm sweats, the current flows through the salt water and the light goes on.'

'You've made a lie detector!' I cried as Gran fastened the tapes on to the headteacher's palms. I noticed the wires

75

ran into her handbag and she kept one hand buried inside it.

Mr Macbeth's smile faded as Gran leaned forward and looked at him. 'You are not the head teacher of Duckpool School, are you?' she asked.

'I am!' he said. The light flashed on and his mouth fell open. He was lying.

'Try again,' Gran said.

'I'm not,' he whispered. The light stayed off. 'I *said* I was the new Head so I could take over the school,' he admitted. 'I planned to make it top of the league and become famous. They'd make me Director of Education and pay me £100,000 a year.'

'Good,' Gran nodded. 'Your real dream was to make money for the Macbeths. You were going to get Duckpool School to the top by cheating, of course. You were going to get rid of Cedric Crump by faking a robbery and letting him get the blame.'

'I asked him to retire,' Mr Macbeth groaned. 'He refused.'

Gran leaned forward suddenly. 'Now tell us what you did with the old headteacher, Mr Ramsbottom.'

'Nothing!' The light flashed. 'I mean . . . We kidnapped him from outside the chip shop in my Jaguar. He's in the shed at the bottom of our garden.'

'Not for much longer,' Gran said. The blue flashing light of a police car reflected down the polished floor of the corridor outside.

Heavy boots tramped towards us. A large constable stood in the doorway. Mr Crump peered past his shoulder. He looked old, tired and scared. 'I'm Detective Constable Laurence Olivier Elloe,' the policeman said.

Gran smiled. 'Hello, L O Elloe,' she said.

Chapter 12

We weren't finished for the evening, of course. First we had to rescue Myrtle Brick from under the vaulting box in the gym. It seems she would have run for the police but she was too weedy to lift the box off her.

'Would you believe it, Myrtle?' Elvis said as he dusted her down and led her out of the school into the cool of the yard. 'Mr Macbeth was a fake. He wanted to take over all the schools in the county!'

'Why?' Myrtle asked in a shivery voice as she pulled her cardigan round her skinny body.

'Because he was greedy!' Elvis explained as they disappeared down the street.

'Why?' Myrtle asked. Sam, Gran and I had to laugh.

We had agreed to go back to the police station to make statements the next day. We turned for home. 'I didn't really have a brick in my handbag,' Gran said. 'It was a Christmas pudding. I told a little fib.'

'You told a bigger fib, Gran,' I said. 'That lie detector was a fake, wasn't it?'

Her eyes twinkled in the orange glow of the street lamps. 'It might have been.'

'You had a switch in your handbag. You knew the truth all along.'

'Might have done. Sometimes you have to cheat a little. Even in science experiments. But you don't have to cheat in those tests next week,' she said. 'When I were a lass I never cheated. Honesty is the best policy. It did me no harm.'

'You came top without cheating?' Sam asked.

'No. I came *bottom*. But at least I were happy. These people like the Macbeths might get to the top – but it will only bring them misery,' she said.

A voice shouted down the street, 'Gertrude?'

We stopped. Mr Crump hobbled down the street towards us. 'They let me go, thanks to you. All thanks to you, I say. I wondered if I might escort you to your home?' he asked.

'It would be an honour,' Gran said.

'It would be an honour for *me*,' the old man said. 'I say, the honour would be all mine!'

Gran blinked. 'That's what I meant!' she cackled and linked his arm.

We went home.

Next day, when we finally got to school, the place was buzzing like a burglar alarm with the news of Mr Macbeth's arrest. We couldn't settle to our lessons.

Miss Trout was trying to teach us Geography with a map of Britain. 'Here we have the border between England and Wales. There is the town of Hay-on-Wye, and there is the town of Ross-on-Wye, here's Preston-on-Wye, Staunton-on-Wye and Monnington-on-Wye. These towns are all on the same river. It is the river . . .???'

The whole class turned to Myrtle Brick. 'Go on, Myrtle. Tell her!'

And Myrtle said . . . 'What?'

Here is a list of all the experiments in this book. Have you tried them all for yourself?

If you have enjoyed this Sparks family adventure, why not try the others in the series?

Book One: Space Race, 0 571 19368 4
Book Two: Chop and Change, 0 571 19369 2
Book Four: Bat and Bell, 0 571 19371 4

These books are available from all good booksellers.
For further information please contact:

The Children's Marketing Department
Faber and Faber
3 Queen Square
London WC1N 3AU

Science Notes

Science Notes

Science Notes

Science Notes